G.I. JOE
AT
IWO JIMA

LOOK FOR THESE OTHER G.I. JOE BOOKS:

G.I. Joe at D-Day

G.I. JOE AT IWO JIMA

James Kelley

SCHOLASTIC INC.
New York Toronto London Auckland Sydney

ISBN 0-590-14979-2

12 11 10 9 8 7 6 5   8 9/9 0 1 2 3/0

Printed in the U.S.A.

First Scholastic printing, March 1998

This book is dedicated to every G.I. Joe who didn't come home from Iwo Jima.

Contents

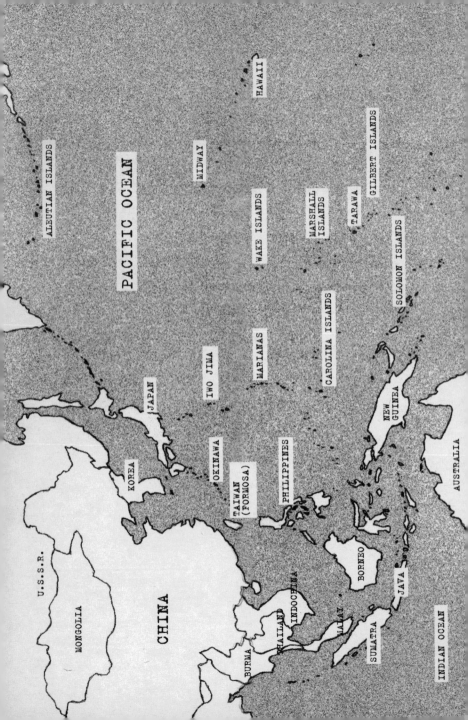

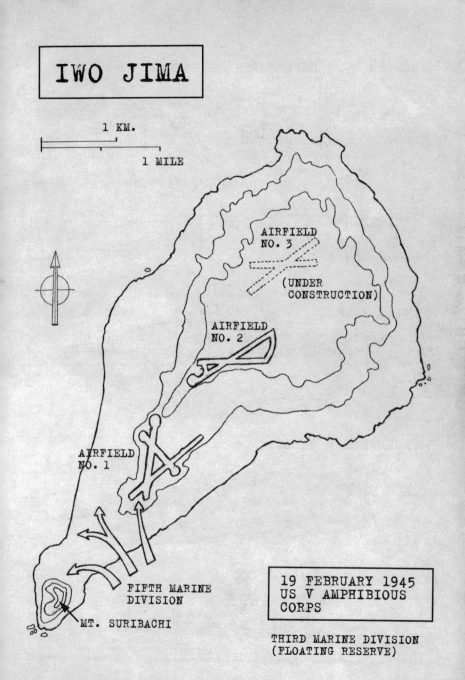

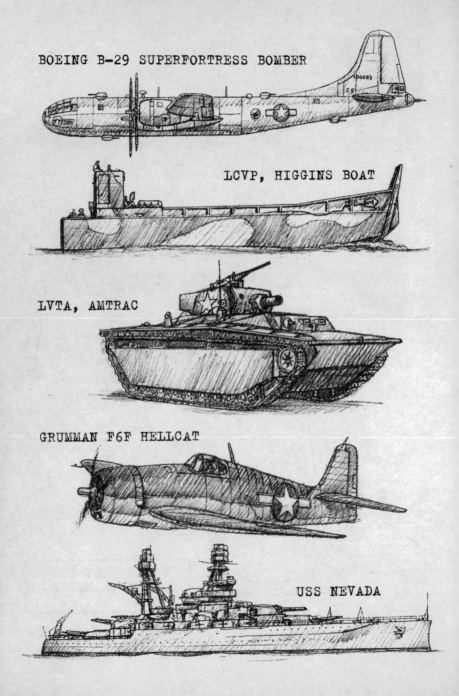

BOEING B-29 SUPERFORTRESS BOMBER

LCVP, HIGGINS BOAT

LVTA, AMTRAC

GRUMMAN F6F HELLCAT

USS NEVADA

COLT
AUTOMATIC PISTOL

HANDGUN
HIP HOLSTER

G.I. JOE®
® & © 1997 Hasbro, Inc.
All rights reserved.

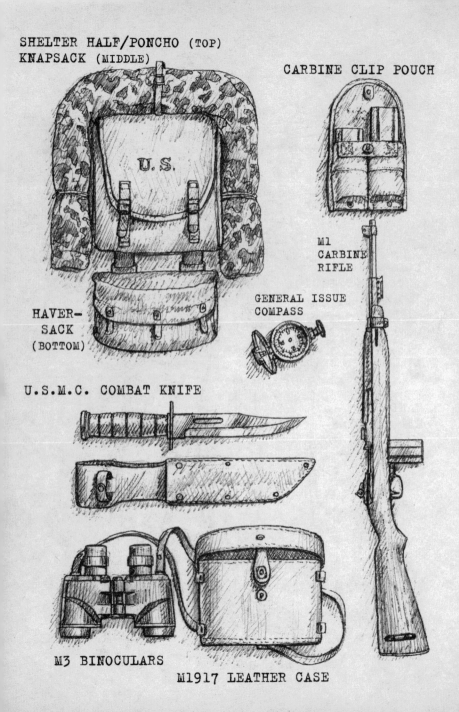

SHELTER HALF/PONCHO (TOP)
KNAPSACK (MIDDLE)

CARBINE CLIP POUCH

U.S.

HAVER-
SACK
(BOTTOM)

GENERAL ISSUE
COMPASS

M1
CARBINE
RIFLE

U.S.M.C. COMBAT KNIFE

M3 BINOCULARS

M1917 LEATHER CASE

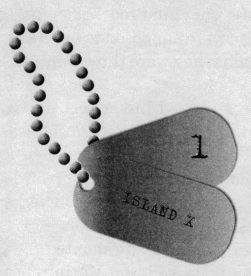

1

ISLAND X

G.I. Joe leaped off the landing craft and dove headfirst into the sand. He heard a loud BOOM! in front of him, and saw a fountain of sand shoot up in the air. He ducked down as a pair of Navy Hellcat fighter planes zoomed just over his head. Then G.I. Joe and the other Marines got up and ran up the beach.

As they reached the first checkpoint, G.I. Joe checked his squad's position. Bad news.

They were one hundred yards north of where they were supposed to be. He looked at his watch. They were three minutes late, too.

G.I. Joe strapped his helmet on tighter and stood up. As the sergeant, he was responsible for making sure his men knew what to do. He waved them forward. The squad had to move up the beach and away from the ships.

"Let's go, you guys!" he shouted.

With a mighty yell, the Marines of Easy Company, led by G.I. Joe's squad, charged up the beach!

G.I. Joe had been training his men for a month. He led them on long hikes and they practiced beach landings.

Amid the swirling smoke, G.I. Joe was not pleased with what he saw. It looked as if his men had forgotten everything he had taught them.

Ronnie "Pete" Peterson had tripped and fallen after jumping off the boat the wrong way. Then two of his fellow Marines ran right past Pete as he tried to get up.

Silvio Pastora had lost his helmet somewhere in the sand, and Dewey Hotchkiss was trying to get untangled from his rifle strap.

John "Gordo" Gordon and Dave "Nails" Nash were running so close together they were stepping on each other's feet.

"Gordo! Nails!" G.I. Joe yelled. "Spread out. And you other guys, help Pete. And Silvio, forget your helmet. Just get up here."

This landing is a disaster, thought G.I. Joe. *Thank goodness it's only practice.*

A loud siren sounded from up the beach. That was the signal that the practice was over.

G.I. Joe marched toward his squad of twelve men. His face was a stony mask.

"Man, I am glad that's over," Silvio said, finding his helmet behind a rock.

"You said it," Pete answered, climbing to his feet. "This was much harder than I thought it would be. These combat boots weren't made for running in sand!"

"You call yourselves Marines?!" G.I. Joe said forcefully. "That was terrible! You've got to work together and move forward steadily. When we're making the real attack, you won't have time to look for lost helmets or fix your rifles."

Silvio and Dewey started to speak, but G.I. Joe cut them off.

"And I don't ever want to see you run past a buddy who has fallen," he said, pointing to Pete, who was still dusting sand off his shirt. "We have to help each other and be a team."

G.I. Joe looked at his men. He didn't like being mean, but as their sergeant, he was responsible for training them. He knew that it was his job to make sure they were ready for battle. This practice attack on the small Hawaiian island of Kahoolawe was just that — practice.

The real thing would come soon. World War II was raging all over the Pacific

Ocean as America battled against Japan. Japan had brutally attacked hundreds of islands and cities. Now it was time to strike back.

Soon G.I. Joe and the Marines would cross the Pacific Ocean to attack a Japanese-held island. The mission was so secret that even G.I. Joe didn't know where the island was. For now, G.I. Joe and his men were calling it Island X.

But as hard as the Marines had been practicing, they weren't ready to take on the battle-hardened Japanese soldiers yet.

I've got to whip these men into shape, thought G.I. Joe. It was a responsibility he took seriously.

G.I. Joe pushed his helmet back on his head. He looked over his squad as they assembled their gear on the beach at Kahoolawe and prepared to move out.

Nails and Gordo had been best friends back in the States. The two Marines had gone to high school together in Idaho and had signed up as soon as they turned eighteen. Since then, they had done everything together.

Silvio was a baker's son from New York City. This tropical weather was strange to a city kid. He had never seen a palm tree until he landed in Hawaii.

Pete was a big-boned farm boy from Kansas. He hadn't been a Marine very long, but he was the proudest guy in the squad.

And Dewey was a brand-new Marine. While G.I. Joe's other soldiers had seen some action, this was Dewey's first real assignment. G.I. Joe knew that he would have to keep a special eye out for this kid.

G.I. Joe had been the squad's sergeant for only a few months. He liked these guys a lot. But he was worried about how they would work as a team in battle.

After a few weeks, G.I. Joe had helped his men become better at their jobs. They were not perfect, but they were much better than that first practice attack on Kahoolawe. They had drilled and trained for days on end. The men of Easy Company were becoming a team.

2

ALOHA MEANS
GOOD-BYE

After a few more weeks of practice in
Hawaii, the orders came down. The ships
would leave for Island X in two days.

It was time to pack up and get ready to
leave.

More than 70,000 Marines would be
making the trip to the island. They
wouldn't find out its name or where it was
until they got close. The invasion was a big

secret; they couldn't let the enemy find out they were coming.

Huge crates of equipment were loaded onto Navy ships. They had to bring everything that they might need with them. There were no supermarkets in the middle of the Pacific Ocean.

The ships were filled with enough food to feed a small city for a month. The Marines packed garbage bags, flares, water barrels, gasoline, batteries, and toilet paper. They even brought food for the search-and-rescue dogs.

After all the supplies were on board, hundreds of vehicles rolled onto special transport ships. G.I. Joe and the squad watched as tractors, bulldozers, rock-crushers, and graders were loaded, along with trucks and jeeps and tanks.

"Say, Sarge," Gordo said as they all leaned on a dock railing watching the building equipment get loaded. "Are we gonna invade an island or build one?"

"We'll do the invading, Gordo," G.I. Joe said. "The Seabees will do the building."

The Seabees were members of the Navy's construction battalions (C.B.s). These soldiers were engineers and construction experts. They built everything from bridges to railroads to airplane runways. But no one knew what they would be building on Island X.

"Let's go, guys, back to the barracks," G.I. Joe said. "We've got our own packing to do."

G.I. Joe directed the men in the squad to check their equipment. Each soldier would carry a wood-and-steel M-1 rifle and two packs of gear. In the packs, they put extra uniforms, a rolled-up blanket, and a rain poncho, along with razors and toothbrushes.

In the pockets of their jackets, they stuffed handkerchiefs, wallets, pictures of loved ones, and other personal items. Some men brought pens and paper.

Onto webbed belts, they clipped extra ammunition and grenades.

It was a lot for one man to carry, but they were Marines. They were used to carrying a heavy load. The U.S. Marines were the men America depended on when they needed a tough job done.

G.I. Joe knew that. That was why he worked so hard to train his men, and why he got mad when they slipped up. He wanted them to be the best they could be. *It's the only way we'll get the job done. And maybe the only way we'll survive,* he thought as he watched them pack.

Early one morning in February 1945, G.I. Joe led his men up the gangplank of a giant transport ship. This would be their home for the long trip to Island X. Along the way, they would learn more about their mission.

The men stowed their packs on the ship. G.I. Joe and his squad gathered on the top deck as the ship pulled away from the dock.

As it headed west away from Hawaii, the sun was rising in the east, behind them.

"That sure is pretty," Nails said.

"I hope we make it back here to see another one," Gordo said quietly. "Aloha, Hawaii."

"Remember, Gordo," G.I. Joe said. "Aloha doesn't just mean good-bye. It also means hello. We'll be back. Just work together, do what we've trained to do, and the next time you say 'Aloha' to Hawaii, it'll mean 'hello.'"

The men watched as the waving palm trees of Hawaii disappeared over the horizon.

Next stop . . . Island X.

3

A MYSTERY
SOLVED

The ships headed across the vast Pacific
toward their mystery destination. G.I. Joe
made sure his men kept in shape with
jumping jacks and sit-ups on deck. It was
crowded, but they wanted to be ready for
the big battle.

They did get some time off to look around
the ship. One day, G.I. Joe and Nails were
walking down a passageway on the boat
when they heard a strange language being

spoken. Nails poked his head into the radio room.

Two Marines were sitting in front of a radio console, speaking into microphones. But Nails couldn't understand a word they were saying.

"Say, Sarge, what language is that, anyway?" he asked.

G.I. Joe had heard it before. "That's Navajo, a Native American language," he said. "No way the Japanese can understand what we're saying."

A few days later, the Marines were gathered on deck for a speech by General Holland "Howlin' Mad" Smith. The fiery Marine general was in command of the entire mission. G.I. Joe made sure his squad was paying attention.

"Men, it's time to tell you where you are going," General Smith said, pointing to a huge map on an easel. The map showed an island that looked like a big teardrop. "This island is called Iwo Jima. It is one of the many Japanese islands. Our mission is to take it away from the Japanese Army." He pronounced the name of the island "EE-woh JEE-ma."

"The trip from Hawaii to Japan is long and dangerous," General Smith continued. "Our B-29 Superfortress bombers need a place to rest and refuel on their way to Japan. If we can capture Iwo Jima, the island will be a base for our bombers."

G.I. Joe's men looked at the map. "It's a speck in the ocean," Pete whispered. G.I. Joe glared at the men to be quiet.

"Your job," General Smith said, "will be to secure Iwo Jima from the Japanese troops that are holding it."

G.I. Joe knew that once the Americans attacked Iwo Jima, the Japanese soldiers would destroy the runways so that American planes couldn't use them. G.I. Joe and the troops would have to make the island safe so the Seabees could do their work.

"Once we control the island," added General Smith, "the Seabees will be able to use the equipment on board to rebuild the airplane runways. Capturing Iwo Jima to use as a base will save the lives of our pilots who would otherwise have to fly much more treacherous missions. And you'll be helping the war end sooner, saving even more lives."

General Smith plucked the cigar from his mouth. His cold, steely eyes stared at each of them.

"It won't be easy," he said. "It might be the toughest thing you'll ever do. But I know you can do it. You're Marines. You're the best fighting men in the world. Your squad leaders will have more details. Dismissed."

Then all the men shouted the Marine Corps motto.

"Semper Fi!"

That is short for *semper fidelis*, which means "always faithful" in Latin. It means that Marines are always faithful to their country and to one another.

Over the next two weeks, as the ships continued toward Iwo Jima, G.I. Joe met with his company commanders. Then G.I. Joe gathered his squad around a large table. A green blanket covered something lumpy. G.I. Joe yanked the blanket off the table, revealing . . .

"A pork chop!" Gordo shouted.

"A catcher's mitt!" yelled Nails.

"An island!" Pete yelled.

"Say, what is this, third grade?" Nails said, taking a closer look at the thing on the table. "This looks like one of those plaster models we built back in school."

"It is a model, Nails," G.I. Joe said. "It's a model of the island we're going to invade. This is Iwo Jima."

The island actually was shaped like a big pork chop. On one edge was a beach. Arrows pointed to where the Marines would land. At a narrow end of the island, a large hill rose up. It was the highest point on the island.

"Boy, if you had a house up there, you'd have a great view," Silvio said, pointing to the hill.

"Silvio, you're going to get a chance to see that view," G.I. Joe said. "Because our job is to capture that hill. If we capture the hill, we will be able to see the Japanese soldiers better. Then we will be able to knock out their guns. And more of our guys will be able to make it onto Iwo Jima safely. But we have to get to the top first."

The men were quiet as they imagined climbing the hill with enemy guns pointed at them. The men knew the invasion was just a few hours away. They would be hitting the beach of Iwo Jima, Island X. And this time it wouldn't be practice. It would be real.

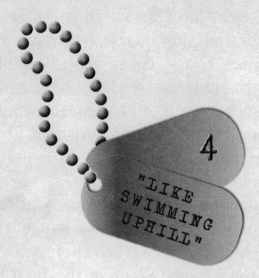

4

"LIKE SWIMMING UPHILL"

At 3 A.M. on February 19, 1945, a bugle blew over the loudspeaker of the Marines' troop ships. The tune was called "Reveille," and meant it was time to get up and get going.

As they always did before an invasion, the Marines had a huge meal of steak and eggs.

By dawn, G.I. Joe had assembled his

men on deck. He showed them where to climb over the side of the transport ship into Higgins boats. These special smaller boats were built to zoom up to a beach, let Marines run off, and then zoom away to pick up more soldiers. Without these sturdy, mobile boats, landing on Iwo Jima would have been impossible.

Several squads were cramped into the Higgins boat with G.I. Joe's squad. The men checked and rechecked their gear, especially their rifles. Some of the men had covered the ends of their guns with plastic bags, to keep sand from clogging their barrels.

As they floated a few miles offshore, a huge noise got louder and louder. BOOM! BOOM! BOOM! over and over and over.

"Man, the Navy is sure giving that island a pounding," Gordo shouted over the sound of the explosions.

"I'm glad they're doing it," Nails said. "That should make our job easier."

"Don't count on it, Nails," G.I. Joe said

between blasts. "The Japanese have built caves and tunnels all over the island. We'll never be able to see them."

Another series of blasts rocked their ears.

The men looked ahead to the beach where they would be landing.

"It's like a giant pinball machine!" Dewey said. "Look at all the lights and flashes!"

He was right. The exploding shells were pinging around the island like pinballs. Bright flashes of orange, red, and yellow sparkled in the distance. But G.I. Joe hoped the young soldier knew that this was no game.

Through the smoke, G.I. Joe could see the 550-foot-tall hill that he would have to lead his men up. They had learned its name last night. Mount Suribachi.

G.I. Joe didn't know it then, but in a few days Mount Suribachi would become one of the most famous places in the world.

*　　*　　*

Just before 9 A.M., the Higgins boats speeded up.

"This is it, boys!" shouted G.I. Joe. He and the other squad leaders on the boat made sure their men were ready. The wind whipped in their faces as the boat sped toward shore. G.I. Joe expected that the Japanese guns would open up on them at any minute.

Now we'll see if I've taught these guys right, thought G.I. Joe. *Now we'll see if they've learned their lessons.*

WHAM! The boat slammed onto the beach. Its wide front doors opened up. With a loud yell, the Marines stormed ashore!

"Let's go, guys, get some cover," G.I. Joe yelled, waving his men onward.

"Hey, how come they're not shooting at us?" Nails shouted as he jumped to the beach.

"What, are you complaining?" Gordo said, running forward.

G.I. Joe checked his watch. Right on time. *These guys are pretty good,* he thought, smiling. *And we're even on the right part of the beach.*

But G.I. Joe's smile soon disappeared. Even though his squad was doing their job well, he saw that they had a bigger problem than Japanese guns.

I can barely move! he realized suddenly.

G.I. Joe was stuck in Iwo Jima's thick, black volcanic sand. It was more like *quick*sand than sand.

He and the other Marines weighed down with heavy packs sank to their knees in the stuff. Footprints filled in immediately. G.I. Joe pulled his shovel from his backpack, but couldn't dig out. Each time he removed a shovel full of sand, more sand rushed in to take its place.

Even lying down and crawling was very difficult.

"This is like swimming uphill," Silvio said as he struggled to pull himself forward.

G.I. Joe looked up and down the beach. Marines were having the same trouble all over. Even trucks were sinking in the slippery sand. The Seabees began to lay out wide wire tracks for the trucks and tractors to roll on. But sometimes even they didn't work, and tractors ground to a halt.

G.I. Joe knew that they had to get up off that beach. If the Japanese started shooting, the Marines would be sitting ducks.

As G.I. Joe slowly moved forward through the thick sand, he saw Gordo and Nails working together to help each other up the beach. He watched Dewey strap his rifle carefully to his back while keeping an eye out for his buddies. Silvio and Pete were using their shovels like oars, pulling themselves up the slippery beach.

G.I. Joe's squad was working as a team. *Practice makes perfect,* he thought.

G.I. Joe's Marines slowly made their way forward, a foot at a time. They had landed half an hour earlier, and they were still not off the beach. It was hard going through the thick sand, but the days and weeks of hiking in Hawaii had strengthened them. They were going to make it.

Suddenly, Japanese guns from the hillside and from hidden bunkers started firing.

The Japanese soldiers had waited for the Marines to get bogged down in the sand.

It was an ambush!

All the men dove to the ground. But for some, that wasn't enough.

G.I. Joe heard Pete yell, and then suddenly he stopped. Pete had been too big a target.

Then Nails grabbed his chest and fell backward into the sand, his helmet rolling away. Gordo jumped to help his friend, pulling him by the arm across the sand. They hid behind a truck that had become stuck in the sand.

"Nails! Nails!" Gordo yelled. "Can you hear me?"

Nails couldn't hear him.

G.I. Joe knew that he had to get his men off the beach . . . *and fast*. They had to find cover in the rocks beyond the black sand. With hundreds of bullets flying around, it would be tough.

But tough was what Marines were made of.

In the face of the enemy guns, G.I. Joe stood up and charged forward as fast as he could in the slushy sand. Inspired by his bravery, other Marines from Easy Company followed, firing their rifles and tossing grenades.

For the rest of the day, the Marines battled forward, inch by inch. Not all of them made it, but they gave their lives for the ones who did.

The battle for Iwo Jima was just starting. It would be a long time before the Marines saw the top of that hill — if they ever would.

5

"WHAT'S THE PASSWORD?"

By the end of the first three days on Iwo Jima, hundreds of Marines were dead and hundreds more wounded. It had been terrible, but in the end, the Marines had come ashore as planned. They had split the island's defenses into two parts.

To the north were the airfields that other Marines would try to capture. To the south, where G.I. Joe was, stood Mount Suribachi.

G.I. Joe gathered his squad at the foot of the hill. The sun was setting over the other side of the island. The moon was only a sliver, and soon the night sky was bright with stars.

Several of the men in the squad had been wounded, and medics worked to patch them up. Others tried to dry off some of their clothes. It was the first time the rain had stopped in two days. They also tried to eat some of the rations they carried with them, but they weren't too hungry.

"We sure ain't in Hawaii anymore," Silvio muttered as he sniffed his beef stew. "I can't believe it. I've never been so miserable in my life."

"You said it," Gordo answered. "And I still can't believe Nails is gone."

G.I. Joe listened as his men talked about their day. But he didn't hear any talk of quitting. *I'm really proud of these guys,* he thought. *This is tough duty, but they're hanging in there. They're great soldiers.*

Not long after the men finished eating, it got even darker as the rain clouds moved back in.

"Okay, men, we'll have to set up camp right here tonight," G.I. Joe said. "I'll assign two-man teams to keep watch for two hours at a time. The rest of you try to get some sleep."

The men huddled near a small hole in the rocks where hot air escaped from the ground. Mount Suribachi was an extinct volcano, but there were still some hot spots inside it. The squad used the heat from the ground for warmth. That was safer than building a fire that would attract attention.

To protect against enemy soldiers sneaking up on them, G. I. Joe ordered his men to string empty food cans on wires around their camp. Anyone who tripped the wires would make a racket that would alert the soldiers.

G.I. Joe and Dewey drew the first watch. The watchful sergeant knew the young soldier might need his help.

After a while, the other men slept. A spooky silence covered the camp. There were none of the usual sounds of night, such as birds or crickets or even wind. There were no birds on the bomb-blasted island because there were no trees for them to nest in. And the only insects were biting black flies that just came out in the daytime.

In the distance, though, G.I. Joe could hear trucks moving through the darkness. Once in a while, the booms of faraway grenades sounded.

"You still awake, Dewey?" G.I. Joe whispered.

G.I. Joe could barely see him across the small campground.

"Yeah, Sarge, I'm still awake," Dewey answered. "I'm so nervous, my eyes are wide open."

"Keep 'em that way," G.I. Joe said. "Remember, these Japanese soldiers like to sneak around at night." For the last two nights, enemy soldiers had made raids on the Marines' camps in darkness.

From his post across the camp, G.I. Joe watched the young soldier carefully. Every little sound made Dewey jump. Gordo rolled over in his sleeping bag and Dewey leaped to his feet. A tractor started up on the beach a few hundred yards away, and G.I. Joe saw Dewey's head spin toward the sound.

Just then, the two men heard the sound of clanking cans. Someone was sneaking up on them!

G.I. Joe poised to move toward the sound. But he waited to see what Dewey would do.

"Halt!" Dewey shouted, pointing his rifle at the sound. "What's the password?" *He's doing just fine,* thought G.I. Joe.

"Roosevelt," said a voice from the darkness. The password for Marines that night was the name of any U.S. president.

"Advance," Dewey said. But like a good

Marine, he kept his rifle up just to be sure. Behind him, G.I. Joe did the same . . . just in case.

A dark form came slowly toward them. Dewey sighted down his rifle. If the form was a Japanese soldier. . . .

Then Dewey and G.I. Joe recognized the green uniform shirt and saw the silver bars of a lieutenant on the collar.

"Easy there, soldier," the Marine lieutenant said. "Any more presidents you'd like me to name?"

Dewey finally relaxed.

"Man, am I glad it's you," he sighed. "I was ready to blast you."

"I'm glad you didn't," the lieutenant said. "Is your squad leader around here?"

"Yes, sir, just a minute," Dewey said quietly. G.I. Joe was right behind him.

"Good job, Dewey," G.I. Joe said. "The men are safe with you on guard."

Dewey beamed. Then he turned back to his watch.

G.I. Joe and the lieutenant moved away to talk quietly.

"New man?" the lieutenant asked.

"He's young," G.I. Joe said, "but he's doing great."

"Nice job, Sarge," the lieutenant said. "Listen, I've got more orders for you from General Smith."

G.I. Joe and the lieutenant talked for a few more minutes. G.I. Joe listened carefully as the officer outlined the mission. Then he handed G.I. Joe a white package, which G.I. Joe stowed in his backpack. The two men saluted each other, and then the lieutenant disappeared into the darkness.

"What did he want, Sarge?" Dewey whispered.

"You'll find out tomorrow," G.I. Joe said mysteriously. "Now go and wake up Silvio to take his turn on watch. And you get some sleep. We'll all need it tomorrow.

"And Dewey," G.I. Joe whispered with a smile. *"Semper Fi!"*

A few minutes later, after he saw that Silvio was in position, G.I. Joe looked upward. The steep slopes of Mount Suribachi loomed over them like a giant shadowy monster.

Tomorrow, G.I. Joe thought, *tomorrow, the Marines have to tame that monster.*

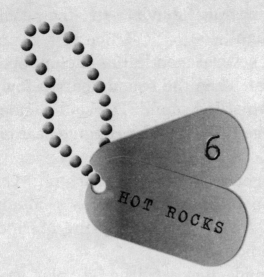

6

HOT ROCKS

The sound of a machine gun woke up G.I. Joe before dawn on February 23. He yelled for his squad to get up and get under cover. Most of the men had slept in their helmets, but those who hadn't grabbed them quickly.

The chattering gun was just above them on the hillside. G.I. Joe could see that it was aiming over his head, toward other

Marines coming ashore in the early morning light.

He saw several men fall as they jumped off the boat. Then the squad heard a high-pitched, whistling sound. The sound ended with a huge BANG! and a Higgins boat exploded.

"We've got to knock out that gun," G.I. Joe said, pointing up the slopes of Mount Suribachi. "We've got to help the Marines who are landing."

The squad quickly gathered their gear and assembled at the bottom of the slope.

"We'll split up," G.I. Joe said. "I'll go with half of the men on one side, the rest of you move around from the other side." He pointed to a spot about fifty yards away.

"Let's go!" he yelled and began clambering up the rocky hillside, followed by Gordo, Silvio, and Dewey. The rest of the squad jogged away to their position.

Climbing the jagged hill was almost as hard as wading through the sand. They grabbed for handholds and tried to keep their feet under them. Silvio fell, but Dewey grabbed him and helped him up.

"C'mon, Silvio," Dewey said. "Keep at it. You can do it."

"What are we, goats?" Silvio said, pulling himself up the hill.

After climbing about one hundred feet, the men neared the machine gun nest. G.I. Joe could just see the gun poking out of a tiny hole in the mountain. He pointed it out to the men.

"Man, Sarge, you were right, they *are* hidden," Gordo said. "I wonder how many more little caves they got in this mountain."

G.I. Joe motioned for them to be quiet. He pointed to the hole in the rocks, and the squad aimed their rifles at the machine gun as G.I. Joe crept up below it. G.I. Joe slipped a grenade off his belt and pulled the pin. As he tossed it into the opening of the machine gun nest, he covered his ears and rolled away downhill.

BLAM!

Rocks and dirt shot out of the hole as the grenade went off.

"That's one machine gun that won't be hitting any more Marines," G.I. Joe said.

He grabbed his rifle and waved the squad onward and upward. "Let's go, guys, we're goin' all the way to the top!"

As the men advanced up the rocky hillside, Gordo suddenly pulled his hand away from a rock he had grabbed.

"Yee-oww!" he said, flapping his hand and blowing on it. "Some of these rocks are hot!"

"This is a volcano, remember?" G.I. Joe said, just up the hill. "Now stop flapping and keep your eye out for snipers."

The squad advanced slowly up the mountain behind G.I. Joe. They checked every cave they found for Japanese soldiers. They saw the craters caused by Navy bombs and missiles.

But they didn't find any Japanese soldiers.

Something's wrong, G.I. Joe thought.

There have to be enemy soldiers up here somewhere.

The men continued upward, foot by foot, constantly alert. At any moment, G.I. Joe expected Japanese soldiers to charge down at them from the top of the mountain.

This is nerve-wracking, G.I. Joe thought. *Why don't they attack?*

G.I. Joe made sure his men's attention didn't wander. But he didn't have to worry too much. After all their practice and all their time together, they were working like a machine. Each soldier was doing his part, keeping an eye out for trouble.

But they didn't find any trouble all the way up Mount Suribachi.

Finally, after about an hour's climb, they found themselves near the top.

G.I. Joe crawled ahead to scout. He discovered that the top of Mount Suribachi was like a giant bowl. *I'm sure glad this volcano can't erupt anymore,* he thought. *But there must be dangers other than lava up here!*

He crawled back down to the men.

"It looks quiet," he said. "But I'm still not sure. We'll all go to the edge and then charge together on my signal."

The men of Easy Company clambered up to the top of the bowl. G.I. Joe knew that while things looked calm, looks could be deceiving. He checked his men's positions.

They were ready. He smiled at Dewey.

"Ready, kid?" he said.

"Let's go, Sarge," Dewey said. "We're with you all the way."

"GO!" shouted G.I. Joe, and the Marines leaped over the top, their rifles ready to meet any threat.

They slid down into the crater and formed a defensive circle, ready to take on any attackers. They were alert as rabbits in a field. They quickly checked the entire area for enemy soldiers.

But the top of Mount Suribachi was as quiet as a crater on the moon.

"Where is everybody?" Gordo wondered.

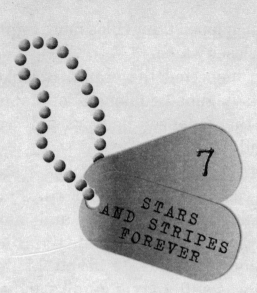

7

STARS
AND STRIPES
FOREVER

"What were we worried about?" Gordo cracked as they stood in the empty crater. "This is easy."

"Hey, this *would* make a great place for a house," Silvio said, admiring the view of the wide, blue sea.

"Quiet, you guys," G.I. Joe hissed. "Be sharp. Remember, the Japanese could be right below us in caves."

The men gripped their rifles more tightly and kept closer watch.

G.I. Joe inspected the crater. It looked like the Navy guns had done a lot of damage. And the Japanese had probably run away to hide.

He peered over the edge of the crater. Below, he could see hundreds of ships just offshore, delivering supplies and more Marines. On the beach, wounded Marines were getting rides back to hospital ships. But there was still a lot of gunfire and explosions.

G.I. Joe knew it was time to follow the orders he had gotten from the lieutenant the night before. First, he had his men secure the top. Now they could see all around the hill and help other Marines with the rest of the attack.

Then it was time to put up an American flag to show that the Marines were in charge now, not the Japanese Army.

Turning back to the men, he pulled the

mysterious white package out of his back-pack.

He opened it to reveal a small red, white, and blue American flag.

"Silvio, Gordo, find me something to hang this on," he said proudly.

The men ran to some Japanese wreckage destroyed by Navy guns. They pried out a long, iron pipe and ran over to their sergeant. They tied the flag to the top of the pole.

"Okay, men," G.I. Joe said. "Let's put 'er up."

As G.I. Joe started to push up the pole, he was startled by a sudden, fierce yell from behind him.

From out of a hidden cave entrance charged six Japanese soldiers, guns blazing!

G.I. Joe's men hit the dirt, looking for cover from the enemy's sneak attack. G.I. Joe saw Silvio get hit and fall. He watched Dewey and several other Marines blast back at the enemy soldiers.

Gordo battled with a Japanese officer who wielded a long sword. The Marine used his rifle and his bare hands to disarm the enemy and then knock him out.

G.I. Joe didn't hit the dirt. He knew that he couldn't let the American flag fall. As the enemy fired at him, he stood tall. He held the heavy pole upright with one hand, while he shot his M-1 at the enemy with the other.

Suddenly, a grenade was launched into the battle from the cave. G.I. Joe saw it arcing from the mouth of the cave toward his men.

He had taken these men too far to let something happen to them now. It was their job to be Marines, but it was his job to protect them if he could. And he had to protect that flag.

Even if it meant his own life.

The grenade was heading right for him! It looked like a big softball . . . but that gave G.I. Joe an idea. He had only seconds to act.

Holding the flagpole with his left hand, he flipped his M-1 around and grabbed the weapon by the barrel.

He eyed the deadly grenade and then swung with all his might. If he missed, he and his squad were doomed.

Like a home run hitter in baseball, G.I. Joe whacked the grenade out of the crater, high in the air.

With a sharp CRACK! it exploded harmlessly in the sky.

The brief battle was over quickly. The squad helped Silvio with his injury and rounded up the Japanese prisoners. They finished raising the flag, securing the pole with rocks piled around the base.

A breeze kicked up and the American flag flapped freely in the wind atop Mount Suribachi.

Offshore, Navy sailors watching in ships cheered the flag. They blew whistles and honked horns. On the beach, Marines whooped and hollered for joy. The Navajo code-talkers flashed word of the flag-raising back to Hawaii. General Smith himself watched from his command post on the black sand with tears in his eyes.

Atop the mountain, G.I. Joe knew that all of his men were thinking of Nails and Pete and the other Marines who had given their lives so that this flag might fly.

I know I'm sure thinking of them, he thought.

G.I. Joe watched as Dewey dug into his backpack and took out a small camera. The young soldier snapped a picture of the Stars and Stripes as it flapped in the wind.

"I bet the families of Pete and Nails would like to see that flag," Dewey said quietly.

G.I. Joe smiled. That was just what he was thinking. That's just what any Marine would think.

Semper Fi, always faithful . . . to one another and to our country.

*   *   *

G.I. Joe and his squad held the top of Mount Suribachi until they were relieved later that day. The new group of Marines brought a larger, ceremonial flag with them. They hoisted the larger flag so that it could be seen for miles around.

As he left the mountain, G.I. Joe saluted the Stars and Stripes.

Mission accomplished.

Then G.I. Joe turned and headed down the mountain. He still had men to lead and more battles to win.

STARS AND STRIPES ON MT. SURIBACHI